MOON SONG

by Byrd Baylor / illustrations by Ronald Himler

Charles Scribner's Sons / New York

Text copyright © *1982 Byrd Baylor*
Illustrations copyright © *1982 Ronald Himler*

Library of Congress Cataloging in Publication Data
Baylor, Byrd.   Moon song.
Summary: After giving birth to Coyote Child and
leaving him to fend for himself, Mother Moon listens for
the moon song of all coyotes.
[1. Coyotes—Fiction. 2. Moon—Fiction] I. Himler,
Ronald, ill. II. Title.
PZ7.B3435Mo   [Fic]   81-18427
ISBN 0-684-17463-4   AACR2

1 3 5 7 9 11 13 15 17 19   Q/C   20 18 16 14 12 10 8 6 4 2
Printed in the United States of America

This book is dedicated with love to
people who are trying to stop government
programs for trapping and poisoning wild animals.
B.B.

Coyote was born
by a brittlebush.
His mother was
the Moon.

Yes, it was here
on Pima Indian land.

Moon came down
from the sky.
You've seen the Moon
move low against the mesa
over there.
You've seen her
touch the earth.
That's how it was
on that cold night.

Beneath that bush
Moon birthed Coyote Child.

She left him there
on hard dry ground,
curled up on rocks,
alone.
She left him in the world
without a thing.

Yes,
she went back to the sky.

She had to go on
with her journey,
working her power,
pulling the tides,
moving the night.
She had to be
at a certain place
across the mountains
by dawn.

Don't blame the Moon.

She couldn't stay.
But at least
she touched Coyote's face
just once
with her pale light.
At least
she wrapped him
in her magic
before she left.

And afterward,
there by Kometke Mountain,
she looked down.

Coyote Child looked up.
He saw his mother
and he wanted her.
He ran across the rocky hills
trying to catch her,
trying to follow,
jumping
and crying
and calling,
Come back!

But the Moon
was always
out of reach.
There wasn't a sound
in the world that night
except
Coyote
howling.

It's true
he was skinny
and hungry
and lonely
and cold.

But
don't worry about Coyote.

Being Coyote,
he lived.

He sniffed the dawn
and greeted the sun
and trotted all over
the Pima world
leaving his tracks...
making trails.

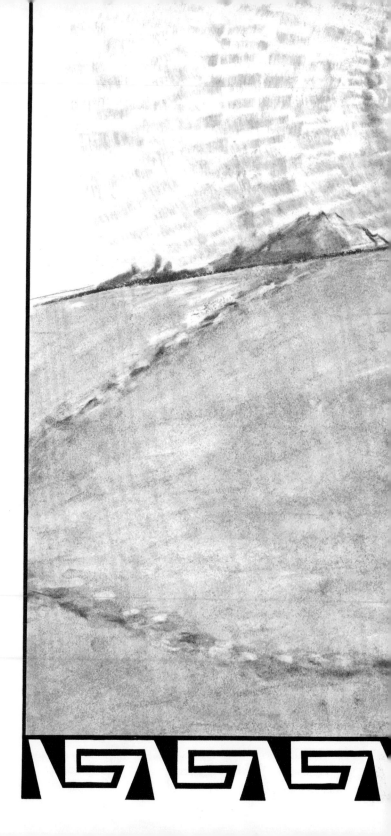

He ran
for the pleasure
of running,
for the pleasure of
looking
around.

That desert child
took care of himself.

He got his strength
from rocks
and wind,
and the dry earth taught him
what he had to know.
He learned it all
in a day.

Yes,
being Coyote,
he felt at home.
Being Coyote,
he lived.

Now
all coyotes
know the things
that First Coyote learned.
They get along
on nothing.
They still speak
a language
Mother Moon
understands.

Look how they gather
in lonely places
on moonlit nights.

They lift their heads
and watch the Moon.
Remembering,
they sing.

There never was
a moon song
as free
and wild
as theirs.
There never was
a moon song
anywhere
as beautiful.

When she hears
that call
the Moon
bends
down.

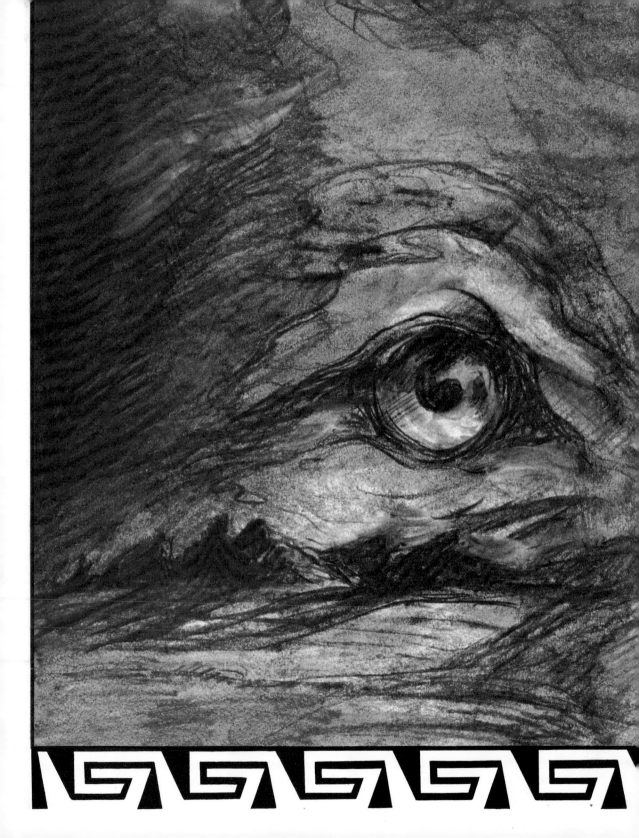

She touches coyotes,
covers coyotes
with pale white mist,
caresses coyotes
wherever they are,
shines
in coyotes' eyes,
fills them with
dreams
and with strange
mysterious
power.

You can tell
something passes
between them...
some secret
the Moon
and coyotes
all know.

Look how
gently
Moon shines
on coyotes.

Moon shines
on coyotes
with
love.

You can tell.